P9-DIE-955

EXPRESS NEWSPAPERS plc, Ludgate House,
245 Blackfriars Road,
London SE1 9UX.

Produced by Brainwaves Limited
5 Highwood Ridge, Hatch Warren, Basingstoke,
Hampshire RG22 4UU.

ISBN 0–85079–249–5

RUPERT

and the
Elfin Bell

'If there's one problem with gardening,'
says Rupert's father one sunny afternoon,
'it's that you have to keep clearing up all
the time!' 'What are we going to do with all
the rubbish we've collected?' asks Rupert.

'I think we'll have a bonfire!' grins Mr
Bear, piling all the branches and twigs up
into a heap. 'Be a good chap and ask Mummy
to bring some matches from the kitchen!' he
asks. When Rupert returns, Mr Bear strikes a
match and carefully lights the bonfire.

Some of the wood and leaves that Mr Bear is burning are still quite damp, and the fire starts to make a lot of smoke. 'Dad?' says Rupert. 'What happens to all the smoke when it goes up into the air?'

Mr Bear is busy tending to the fire, 'It just blows away, Rupert,' he says. 'But where does it blow *to*?,' asks Rupert again, determined to get an answer. ''That's an interesting question,' says Mr Bear. 'I've never really thought about it!'

Disappointed at not getting an answer, Rupert goes to help his Mother clear up the garden. 'Do you know where smoke goes to?' he asks her as he rakes up some leaves. 'No dear,' she replies, 'I'm sorry, I don't.'

Just then Bill comes to the garden gate. 'Can Rupert come and play in the woods?' he enquires. 'Can I Mum?' asks Rupert. 'Of course,' agrees his mother. 'But be back in good time for tea, I'm making fresh scones!' she says, smiling.

The pals run off towards Nutwood Forest.
'Do you know where smoke goes to?' Rupert
asks Bill. 'Neither of my parents have any
idea.' 'No,' replies Bill. 'I'll just have
to ask our teacher when we go back to school
tomorrow!' says Rupert.

Coming over the top of a hill, the pals see
smoke coming from the woods. 'Somebody has
lit a bonfire down there!' cries Bill. 'I
wonder who it can be?' says Rupert. 'Let's
go and find out!'

Reaching the woods, the pals set out to
find where the smoke is coming from. Through
the trees they spot a figure. 'That looks
like our gipsy friend Rollo!' says Rupert.
'I wonder if that smoke came from his fire?'

'Hello Rupert!' grins Rollo when he sees the
pals. 'Granny and I have just arrived – I'm
collecting some wood so we can cook a meal!'
'So that smoke we saw doesn't come from your
fire?' asks Bill. 'No,' says Rollo, 'I
haven't lit it yet!'

Seeing the puzzled expression on the pals' faces Rollo asks, 'What's the matter?' 'Well if it's not your fire, then who's is it?' says Rupert.

'Let's go and find out!' says Rollo, and the three friends go off in search of the mystery smoke. They're about to give up, when Rollo cries out 'I've found it! But it isn't a bonfire at all!' Running to where Rollo is standing, Rupert and Bill are amazed to see smoke pouring out of a rock!

'This is very strange,' says Rollo, 'I've never seen anything like this before – we'd better go and see my old Granny, perhaps she'll know what's going on.'

Rupert and Bill follow Rollo back to his caravan. 'Hello Rupert!' says Granny, when they get there. 'We wondered if you knew anything about the smoke we've seen coming out of the ground?' asks Ruper. 'Wait a minute,' she smiles knowingly, 'and I may be able to help you . . .'

Rollo's Granny goes back into the caravan.
Waiting outside the pals can hear her moving
things about. 'What can she be looking for?'
wonders Rupert.

When Granny reappears at the door of the
caravan Rupert can see that she's got
something quite small in her hand. Smiling,
she holds up a tiny, golden bell and says;
'You must ring this where the smoke is
thickest, Rupert. Only then will you find
the answer to your question!'

Saying goodbye to Rollo, who still has to
collect the wood for his own fire, Rupert
and Bill set off back to the smoking rock.
'I wonder what will happen when we ring the
bell?' says Rupert.

Standing on the rock, with the thick smoke
curling up around him, Rupert shakes the
bell, which makes a magical, tinkling sound.
'Look!' cries Bill, as a little elf appears
out of the smoke. 'Where did *he* come from –
and why is he holding a spanner?'

Leaping up on to the rock, the little elf asks the pals what they want. 'You've called me away from a *very* important job,' he says, waving his spanner in the air. 'I've got to mend a broken smoke pipe, but it's much too big a job for me!'

As Rupert and Bill look on astounded, the elf explains that what he really needs is for someone to go to elf headquarters and get more help. 'I *must* stay here and try my best to put things right!' he says.

'Perhaps we can help?' suggests Rupert.
'We'd be very happy to,' agrees Bill. 'As
long as we're back in time for tea . . .' he
whispers to Rupert.

'Oh that would be wonderful!' says the elf.
'Come with me and I'll show you what to do.'
Taking the two friends over to a big flat
rock, he asks them to sit down on it. 'Wait
just a second,' he tells them. 'I won't be
long – and hang on tight!' 'I wonder where
he's going to?' says Bill.

'Do you think this is a good idea?' Bill asks Rupert as they wait patiently on the rock. 'Don't worry,' replies his pal, 'I'm sure we'll find out soon enough what the elf wants us to do!'

The next thing they know the pals hear the clanking of machinery, and the rock they're sitting on begins to tip forward. 'Crikey!' yells Bill. 'Oh no!' cries Rupert, as they both lose their grip and fall into a deep, dark hole . . .

'We seem to be in an underground tunnel!'
coughs Rupert, picking himself up. 'But I
can't see a *thing* because of all this
smoke!' 'Well that elf might have told us
what was going to happen!' complains Bill.

'Sorry if I frightened you!' says the elf.
'Now climb into this,' he carries on,
pointing to a small railway car, 'and take
my cap badge to show the guards at the other
end of the tunnel. Otherwise they won't know
you're on elf business!'

Explaining that the rail-car will take them
straight to elf headquarters, the elf shows
Rupert how it works. 'This handle controls
your speed,' he says, 'pull to go faster,
and push to stop – it's very simple!'

'I hope there are no more nasty surprises!'
says Bill, his voice muffled by the
handkerchief he's holding in front of his
face because of the smoke. 'I'm glad we're
on rails,' says Rupert. 'I'd never be able
to steer otherwise!'

Rupert pulls back the handle and the car
begins to speed along the tracks. 'Wheee!'
cries Rupert, as the little car clatters
round a curve. 'This is just like a ride at
the fun fair!' 'I prefer the coconut shy
myself,' says Bill.

As the smoke clears the pals see a distant
speck of light, which starts to grow bigger
and bigger. Soon they can tell that the
tunnel is coming to an end, 'You'd better
slow down now,' Bill warns Rupert.

Rupert brings the rail-car to a halt just as
it comes out of the tunnel. Waiting for them
is a small elf wearing a smart uniform and a
peaked hat. 'Who goes there!' he shouts,
pointing at the pals. 'And what are you
doing using our private railway?' demands
another guard, rather gruffly.

'Not a very friendly welcome,' whispers
Bill, as Rupert starts to get out of the
rail-car, 'considering we've come all this
way to do them a favour!'

Rupert shows the guard the badge he's been given by the elf, as well as the little bell. 'There's a terrible leak of smoke under Nutwood Forest!' he says. 'Why didn't you say you were sent by one of our elves!' smiles the guard.

'I'm sorry if I was rude,' the guard elf continues. 'We don't get many strangers here. But as you're trying to help us we must get you on your way to headquarters as soon as possible – follow me!'

Leading Rupert and Bill to the top of a
hill, the guard points towards a castle
surrounded by mist, 'There it is,' he says
proudly, 'Elf H.Q.!' 'But how on earth are
we going to get to it?' asks Bill. 'We'll
never find our way in that fog!'

'The mist is there to protect us and stop
ordinary people from finding our
headquarters,' explains the guard. 'But you
have an elfin bell, so you shouldn't have
any problems getting there!'

Clambering down a steep path, the two
pals eventually find themselves surrounded
by thick, swirling mist on the floor of the
valley. 'Which way do we go now?' asks Bill,
looking all around.

'I *think* it's this way,' says Rupert. 'At
least I hope it's this way . . .' he goes on,
as he and Bill walk into the thick fog.
Then, looming up out of the mist, they see a
dark, towering cliff-face. Rupert sighs, 'We
must be lost after all . . .'

'The guard said we'd be all right because we have an elfin bell,' says Bill as they look for a way out of the valley, 'so why don't you ring it and see what happens?' 'What a good idea Bill!' exclaims Rupert, stopping to get the bell out of his pocket. 'Why didn't I think of that before!'

Rupert rings the bell, and the pals wait anxiously as its clear note dies away. Then, from somewhere high above, they hear another bell. 'Someone's heard us!' cries Bill.

Way up in the mist, Rupert and Bill suddenly hear the noise of something moving. 'What can that be?' wonders Bill, peering as hard as he can through the fog to see if he can spot anything.

Then slowly from out of the gloom they see a strange chair appear, swinging down towards them on the end of a long rope. 'How odd,' says Rupert. 'I wonder where that's come from?' 'I'm not at all sure about this . . .' frowns Bill.

'This looks like the only way out,' says
Rupert. 'I'll go first and see where it
takes me!' He climbs in, fastening the
safety bar, and with a lurch the chair
slowly lifts off the ground.

When the chair reaches the top Rupert finds
an elf waiting there, 'Who are you?' he
demands. 'I must get to see your Chief!'
says Rupert, showing him the cap badge. 'But
please don't forget to send the chair back
for my friend Bill!'

Rupert follows the elf into a passage and they run along it until they come to a door. 'The Chief's in there,' says the elf, 'I'll just unlock the door and we'll go in!'

As the door swings open, Rupert is amazed to see inside a brightly-lit room full of dials, switches and humming machinery. 'My goodness,' he thinks, as he walks in, 'what an incredible place!' Just then he notices someone sitting behind a big desk. 'That's our Chief!' whispers the little elf.

Rupert tells the Chief about the broken pipe under the forest in Nutwood, and the whole story of how he and Bill used Granny's elfin bell to try and find out where the smoke was coming from.

Running over to a large, complicated machine, the Chief presses some buttons and pulls a lever, 'You're right!' he exclaims, looking worriedly at the screen in front of him. 'We must send a repair team straight away, that's a very bad leak indeed!'

Speaking quickly into a microphone, the
Chief asks for a repair team to be assembled
as swiftly as possible. 'I want six of our
best mechanics, with their toolkits – this
is urgent!' he orders.

Taking Rupert with him, the Chief then goes
out of the control room to where the repair
team have lined up. Reading from notes he
has taken while Rupert was talking, the
Chief gives the team instructions on how to
get to the broken pipe.

As they watch the repair team disappear into the mist, on their way to fix the broken pipe, Rupert suddenly hears his name being called. Turning round he sees Bill running towards him.

'Hello Rupert,' he calls, 'I *am* glad to see you!' 'I was wondering where you'd got to,' says Rupert. 'What happened?' Bill explains that he had to wait for the elf to get back from taking Rupert to the Chief, 'But I'm here now, so that's all right!' he says.

Now that they have completed their job,
Rupert can't resist asking the elves what
all the pipes running under the forest are
for. 'And what do you do with all that
smoke?' he enquires.

'That's a good question!' beams the Chief.
'I'll get someone to come and take you for a
guided tour!' Moments later another elf
appears and asks them to follow him.
'Perhaps now I can find the answer to my
question!' Rupert says to Bill.

The elf takes them off to a very long escalator, and as it moves them very slowly upwards the pals stare at miles and miles of creaking, hissing pipework. 'It's like a massive steam engine!' says Bill, as he peers around him.

'Smoke is our business!' says the elf as they near the top of the stairs. 'But I can explain everything much better when we get up on the roof – there's so much more to see up there!'

Coming out onto the roof, the two pals are
dumbfounded by what they see. All around
them are huge, whirring fans. 'What on
earth?' says Bill, not believing his eyes.

'These fans,' explains the elf, 'suck in all
the smokey air and send it down below. We
then take all the smoke out of it and send
the clean air back!' 'But what happens to
the smoke?' asks Rupert, still puzzled.
'Once it's been removed from the air we turn
it into mist and fog!' beams the elf.

'So *that's* what happens to all the smoke!'
beams Rupert, delighted to have finally
found the answer to his question. 'Don't you
think it's about time we were going home?'
says Bill. 'I'm getting rather hungry, and
it must be nearly time for tea.'

Their guide says he knows a short-cut to
Nutwood, but just as he's showing them into
a lift, he's called away to help a smoke
engineer who has a problem. 'Wait a second,'
he tells the pals. 'I won't be long!'

While they're waiting for the elf to return, Rupert and Bill decide to have a peek inside the lift. 'I'm sure they won't mind,' says Bill, looking around at all the levers, pulleys and switches.

'Don't touch anything,' warns Rupert. 'We don't know what any of these things do, and it all looks rather complicated to me!' But he's too late! Before Rupert can stop him, Bill flicks one of the switches on the wall. 'I wonder what this one does?' he says.

Before they can get out of the lift the two pals hear the high-pitched whine of a motor starting up. Then the floor suddenly falls away beneath them, leaving the controls behind – and out of reach! 'Oh no!' cries Rupert. 'My feet have left the ground we're dropping down so fast!'

'Sorry Rupert . . .' says Bill as they fall, picking up speed by the second, 'I didn't know this was going to happen – I hope it's a soft landing!'

The lift finally comes to a halt with a
Bump! Picking themselves up, the pals
discover that there are no switches at the
bottom of the shaft to allow them to return.
'We'll just have to go outside and see where
we are,' says Rupert.

Cautiously pushing the door open, the two
friends find themselves in the mist-filled
valley once more. 'I do believe we're back
where we started!' says Rupert. 'Yes,'
agrees Bill, 'lost again!'

Wandering through the fog, with no idea
where they are, Rupert and Bill eventually
stumble across a large tree. 'We haven't
seen this before,' says Rupert, 'No . . .' says
Bill. 'But I'm not sure we'd recognise it
even if we had!'

'Let's climb up as high as we can,' suggests
Rupert. 'Then we might be able to see
something!' 'We could try calling for help
too,' says Bill, wishing that he'd left the
switch in the lift well alone.

Even from the top of the tree the pals still can't see much, as the mist appears to be getting thicker. 'Hello!' cries Rupert, 'Can *anyone* hear me out there?' 'It's no use,' moans Bill, 'we'll *never* be found!'

They begin to clamber back down the tree and are surprised to hear a voice from amongst the branches. It's their elf guide! 'I guessed you must have touched a switch,' he grins. 'So I came after you – I heard your calls, but I thought I'd surprise you!'

The little elf leads Rupert and Bill back
along the valley towards the railway line.
'You'll soon be back in Nutwood!' he says
merrily. 'We've already turned the rail-car
around so it's ready for you!'

In a matter of moments the elf leads them out
of the mist and as soon as the railway guard
sees them he stands smartly to attention.
'He's saluting!' says Bill. 'I think the
elves must be pleased with all the help
we've given them,' replies Rupert.

'Right!' says their guide. 'Climb aboard –
you remember how to work the rail-car, don't
you Rupert?' 'Oh yes,' says Rupert. 'Just
don't go too fast round corners!' says Bill.

The guide gets in behind the two pals, and
pulling the control lever gently back,
Rupert sends the rail-car speeding towards
Nutwood. 'Hello!' cries the first elf they
had met, as Rupert brings the car to a halt
under the forest. 'You two have really saved
the day!'

'Thanks to you we've nearly finished mending
the pipe!' the elf tells Bill and Rupert.
Somewhere down the tunnel the pals can hear
the *squeak!* of screwdrivers and the *bang!* of
hammers as the repair team work away
furiously to complete their task.

'How are you going to get us back above
ground?' asks Bill. 'Sit on that flat rock,'
says the mechanic, going over to a lever,
'and we'll get you on your way before you can
say "Mist and fog" – hold on tight!'

With a *Hiss*! and a *Whoosh*! the rock swings
upwards and the pals and their guide
suddenly find themselves in the bright
sunlight 'Oof!' says Bill. 'Crikey!' says
Rupert, as they both fall over backwards
with surprise.

'Goodbye!' says their guide, 'and here's
your elfin bell, don't forget to give it
back to Rollo's Granny!' 'What an adventure!'
says Bill, as the friends run back through
the woods to Rupert's house.

As they run up the garden path the two pals sniff the air. 'Ah!' sighs Rupert. 'Fresh scones for tea!' 'I could eat a hundred!' grins Bill, rubbing his tummy, which is rumbling quite loudly by now.

Coming into the house they meet Rupert's father. 'I know what happens to smoke now!' cries Rupert. 'The elves clean it out of the air and send it back as mist and fog!' 'Well I never!' chuckles Mr Bear. 'You learn something new every day!'